God
Made You Beautiful!

Written By: Stephanie Farley

Illustrated By: Lisa Powell Braun

How beautiful you are, my darling! Oh, how beautiful!

Song of Solomon 1:15

I dedicate this book to little girls everywhere of every size, shape and color. You are beautiful in His sight. I also want to dedicate it to my amazing husband and my two beautiful children- Amanda and Collin. God has blessed me beyond measure with your love.

Sometimes I like to pretend I am a princess. I get dressed up in fancy clothes and carry a sparkly wand.

And sometimes I like to play dress up and have tea parties in my room.

Mommy says it's fun to pretend,
but to remember that God made
me beautiful just like I am.

You wove me together in my mother's womb. Psalm 139:13

And that I don't need fancy clothes and bows in my hair to be beautiful.

You are altogether beautiful, my darling, beautiful in every way.
Song of Solomon 4:7

God makes all different kinds of people. There's no one in the entire world that looks just like me.

The human body has many parts, but the many parts make up one whole body. So it is with the body of Christ.

1 Corinthians 12:12

And I think that's good, because it would be pretty boring if we all looked the same.

How strange a body would be if it only had one part! It takes many parts to make a single body. That's why the eyes cannot say they don't need the hands. That's also why the head cannot say it doesn't need the feet.

1 Corinthians 12:19-21

Mommy says God made me on purpose and every freckle is right where it was meant to be.

But our bodies have many parts, and God has put each part just where He wants it.

1 Corinthians 12:18

We are all beautiful in God's eyes. Just the way we are...

God created men and women to be like Himself. He gave them His blessing and called them human beings.

Genesis 5:1-2

9 781609 578268